SECRETS

SECRETS

Patricia Scanlan

BBC
LARGE
PRINT

First published in 2006 by
New Island
This Large Print edition published
2009 by BBC Audiobooks
by arrangement with
New Island

ISBN 978 1 405 62249 3

British Library Cataloguing in Publication Data available

Printed and bound in Great Britain by
CPI Antony Rowe, Chippenham, Wiltshire

One

'My heart is low, my heart is so low, as only a woman's heart can be . . .' Kate Ryan sang as she wiped her grey and white marble worktops. The woman who had written that song knew *exactly* what Kate was feeling at that moment. Low, fed up, depressed and very worried.

When Kate was stressed she cleaned her worktops over and over again. The bread bin and matching set of coffee, tea and sugar containers were wiped until they were spotless. The tiles by the sink and cooker were polished until they gleamed. Today the worktops were getting a good going over. So were the fridge-freezer doors and the top of the cooker.

Kate always headed for the kitchen when she was under pressure. Her sister attacked the bathroom in her moments of stress. Kate's best friend, Anna, cut the grass.

Stress was a great way to get the house and garden jobs done, she thought glumly. She squirted more Mister Muscle onto her cooker top. And boy did Kate feel under stress. Her husband, Bill, had been out of a job for the last eighteen months. There was no sign of anything coming up. Christmas was just a week away.

Her three children were up to ninety with excitement, waiting for Santa's arrival.

The Christmas shopping had to be done. She and Bill had just had a row about it. And to crown it all, she'd had a call from a friend she hadn't seen for three years to say she would be home for Christmas. She wanted to visit the day after Stephen's Day.

Kate gave a sigh that came from her toes. Normally she loved having visitors. It would have been a pleasure to see Carmel, her old school friend. But these days, she didn't want to see anyone. She just wanted to shrivel up inside her shell and stay there. In the last few months, all her hope that Bill would easily find another job was fading. As money got tighter their savings dwindled. Kate felt like burying her head in the sand like an ostrich.

She didn't want Carmel Clancy coming to her house when she had no oil for the central heating. Kate didn't want her friend to know that she'd had to sell her car because they needed the money. Bill's Golf was in the garage because they hadn't the money to tax and insure it.

Carmel would have to put up with turkey and ham leftovers because that's all she'd be getting. Kate just didn't have the money for smoked salmon, sun-dried tomatoes and the like. It was eighteen months since she'd been able to afford luxuries like that.

Kate rubbed at a stubborn piece of

grit. It was embedded between the edge of her drainer and the worktop. To think she couldn't even afford to go to a deli any more. Who would ever have thought it? Who would have ever thought that their comfortable lifestyle would have gone from under them?

She still felt sick as she remembered Bill telling her that the multi-national computer company he worked for was closing its Irish operation. Five hundred jobs were gone. He was grey faced and shaken.

'I'm finished, Kate. I'll never get another job at my age.' Her husband sat with his head buried in his hands. Kate tried to take in what he had just told her.

'Don't be daft, Bill! You're only forty-one. That's young. Companies are always going to need human resource managers. *Experienced* human resource managers.' She tried to keep the shake out of her voice. Bill needed her to be strong and reassuring. This was not the time for panic.

'Kate, you don't know what it's like out there. I'm telling you, it's cutthroat. They can get chaps half my age, with better degrees, who'll work for less than my salary because they're so desperate to get a job.' Bill had tears in his eyes. Kate was horrified at the state her usually cheerful and easygoing husband was in. She flung her arms around him and hugged him tightly.

'Stop worrying, Bill. We'll manage fine. You'll get a job. I know you will. You're the best there is. You'll be snapped up in no time,' she comforted, believing every word she spoke. Bill was bloody good at his job and just the best there was. He'd get another job—and soon.

Week after week, month after month, she'd said the same thing over and over. She tried hard to keep their spirits up. Unemployment didn't happen to people like her and

Bill. They had a pretty three-bedroom semi-detached dormer bungalow in a lovely tree-lined estate in Bray. They had always been able to afford a fortnight in the sun every year. There had been music and swimming lessons for the kids. Jaunts to McDonald's. Meals out for her and Bill. It had all been available. Kate had never thought that it would ever be otherwise.

When she had thought about unemployment, before it touched her own life, she had an image of people in the inner city or the more run-down suburbs. People whose lifestyles were very different from her own. Kate wasn't a snob or anything like it. She was lucky and she knew it. She'd never thought that unemployment could affect her family. Bill was a trained professional with years of work experience. Being a human resource manager for a staff of five hundred employees was an important job.

People like him didn't end up on a dole queue. Or so she'd thought.

'Get real, Kate!' her younger sister, Sally, said a few months after Bill had been made redundant. Kate had been moaning about their situation. Sally was a community welfare officer and knew a lot about unemployment.

'Don't kid yourself that it's all people from so-called deprived areas that are on the dole. It isn't. There are a hell of a lot of people like Bill, in middle management, who are out there suffering behind their lace curtains. They go to the St Vincent de Paul for help with their mortgage repayments. People who enjoyed a lifestyle just like yours.'

'St Vincent de Paul? But that's for people who need help,' Kate said, horrified.

'These people *do* need help,' Sally said gently. 'They are living in lovely houses, with no heating and no phones and not enough money to pay the ESB bill and the mortgage. They live in fear of their homes being repossessed. They need help too.'

Seeing Kate's stricken face, she said kindly, 'Look, I'm not suggesting you're ever going to need to go to the St Vincent de Paul. But what I *am* saying is start economising. Use some of Bill's redundancy money to whack a bit off your mortgage. Get rid of one of the cars. I'm not saying that Bill won't ever get a job again. Hopefully he will. But don't think that he's going to swan into a new position just like that. It doesn't happen that way any more, unfortunately.'

Kate came away from her chat with her sister more scared than she had ever been in her life. For the first time since the redundancy had happened, she had lifted her head out of the sand and taken a long, hard look at their situation. Sally's words might have been harsh, but they stiffened Kate's resolve. It was time to sit down, take stock and face the facts. Bill was unemployed and likely to stay that way. The future had to be faced.

Two

That night, when the children were in bed, Kate sat down with Bill. She calmly announced that it was time for them to make long-term plans. Her husband slumped at the kitchen table and lit a cigarette. She could see his fingers shaking.

'I don't know how we're going to manage,' he muttered.

I'd like to kill the bastards that caused this, Kate thought angrily as she saw his hopes and dreams fade to ashes. He took out his calculator and they began to work on the figures he had in front of him.

Bill said they had to reduce their mortgage by two-thirds. That was vital. At least they would know that their home was safe enough then. They would use his lump sum to accomplish that. Then they would sell her car. With the money they would make from that, they'd continue to pay the insurance policies for as long as they could. The most important of these was the policy they had taken out for their children's education. They would pay the VHI for another year. If Bill didn't get a job by then, there would be no more private health insurance.

They went to bed very subdued.

Kate began to take her calculator to the supermarket. She had never considered the cost of food much before. She had put whatever she wanted into the trolley. But those days were gone. Now it was coming up to the second Christmas of Bill's unemployment. Her money was cut to the bone. Any saving, no matter how small, was welcome.

Thank God for big impersonal supermarkets, she thought one day as she stood at the cash desk with her trolley full of own-brand goods. It would be a bit embarrassing if the neighbours saw her. Or if the girl at the checkout knew her.

It wasn't that she normally cared what people thought of her. It was just that these days she seemed to be more vulnerable. Only the other day, her son Matthew had come into the kitchen. His seven-year-old face was scarlet with anger and confusion.

'Mammy, Jason Kent says that Daddy's got no job and that we're going to be poor. He says you can't afford to bring us to EuroDisney. He's a big liar, isn't he? I told him to put his dukes up and I gave him a puck in the snot. He went home bawling,' Matthew added with immense satisfaction.

'That wasn't very nice, Matthew,' Kate said, hoping that Jason Kent's nose was well and truly bloodied. Little brat. Since the Kents had moved in next door, six months ago, there had been nothing but fights with the youngsters on their street. It wasn't really Jason's fault. It was that horrible father of his, Owen.

Owen Kent was the most big-headed, boastful, snobby man Kate had ever had the bad luck to meet.

Owen was a broker, who had begun to make good money. He was on the way up and he liked to boast. He and his wife, Jill, and their two children, Jason and Gemma, had moved into the house next door last summer. They had proceeded to make themselves very unpopular with their neighbours. At first, the six other families on their street had welcomed them. They had been friendly and polite. Gradually Owen's boastful ways had begun to grate.

It was his 'I'm a broker. What do you do for a living?' carry-on that got under people's skin. Owen had the biggest satellite dish, the biggest barbecue pit, the most expensive shrubs. If any of the neighbours bought something new, Owen couldn't bear to be outdone. He would get the same item—except bigger. He *loved* boasting. And he always made sure that when he was bragging to someone, the other neighbours could hear as well.

Kate did not usually make snap judgements about people. But she knew very soon after she met Owen that she couldn't stand him.

Late one afternoon, she had been sitting out the front sunbathing and watching her three-year-old daughter. Jessica was playing on the lawn with a friend. They were having a tea party with her toy tea set. They were sitting on an old tartan rug having great fun. Kate, drowsy and lazy from the heat, had pushed all her problems to the back of her mind. She was content to enjoy the afternoon sun.

She lay on her lounger and felt a rare sense of well being and peace. In the distance she could hear Matthew and Rachel, her other children, playing with their friends nearby. A bee buzzed slowly by. A lark opened his throat and sang his little heart out. Bill had gone into Dublin on the DART to check out the employment agencies. He wouldn't be home for ages. These precious few hours were her own. Kate's limbs twitched as she sank deeper into relaxation. She was just about to drift off into sleep when a monstrous, whining drone jerked her to wakefulness. Owen was out with his petrol-driven lawnmower. It was, of course, a state-of-the-art lawnmower, but Kate was not impressed. Her lovely, peaceful afternoon was ruined.

'Hello there. Catching a few rays? Jill's out the back on the new swing lounger we bought. You should get one. They're great,' he said cheerily as he began to zoom up and down his lawn with the mower.

Smart ass, thought Kate sourly as she gave a polite wave. He knew very well that Bill wasn't working and that they didn't have money to splash out on swinging loungers. She watched him between her lowered eyelids. You'd think it was the Botanic Gardens he had to mow with his petrol lawnmower. All he had was a little hanky of green that the rest of them managed to mow with electric mowers. The *noise* of it.

'Jill's trying to get a tan before we take off to Malta next week. She wants to be able to head right out into it. I've told her she should go and get a spray tan. The sun here just isn't strong enough,' Owen announced as he took a short rest.

'Hmm,' Kate murmured politely. *Bullshitter*, she thought privately. She closed her eyes again, hoping he would take the hint. Five minutes later, he was zooming around her front lawn, which adjoined his in the open-plan manner.

'Might as well do yours while I have the machine out,' he said briskly, coming right up beside her lounger.

'It's OK. Bill will take care of it,' she said hastily, pulling up her boob tube, which had slipped a bit.

'It's no bother,' Owen said. 'Besides, it will save you a bit on your electricity.'

Kate's cheeks flamed. The cheek of him! The utter *cheek* of him. Who the hell did he think he was, going on about her electricity? They weren't paupers. Kate was furious. It was as bad as the day Jill had invited her in for coffee.

Jill with her heavily made-up face and her perfectly manicured nails. She made sure to let Kate know that she had a woman who came in to clean twice a week. She had timed the coffee invitation with the arrival of the woman who did her ironing.

Jill's daughter Gemma was the same age as Jessica. As the two women sat drinking freshly ground coffee, Jill paused in their conversation and said sweetly, 'I wonder if I have anything I could give you for Jessica. She and Gemma are the same age and Gemma has *so* many clothes. I've got lots of stuff that she's never worn.'

Kate was stunned. She'd only met the woman twice, for heaven's sake. And here she was offering her clothes for Jessica. Did she think the Ryans were on their uppers just because Bill was unemployed?

Kate assured her new next-door neighbour that Jessica had plenty of clothes. She hastily finished her coffee and made her escape. Even if Jessica had to go around in rags, she wouldn't accept such impertinent charity from the superior Kents.

'If you just move your lounger and the girls' rug I'll be finished in a jiffy,' Owen ordered as he mowed vigorously.

'Thank you, Owen, but if you don't mind leaving it, Bill will finish it off. I'm just relaxing here,' Kate said coolly. She'd had just about enough of the boastful, intrusive Owen Kent for one afternoon.

'Well, if you're sure,' Owen said, taken aback that she wasn't falling all over him with gratitude.

'I'm sure. Thank you,' Kate said curtly.

'Fine. Enjoy yourself,' he said stiffly, moving off with injured dignity. Two minutes later, he was mowing his other neighbour's lawn. Like a bloody dog marking his patch, Kate thought grimly as she lay back against her cushions.

You weren't very neighbourly, she accused herself silently as she tried to regain her previous sense of relaxation. Was she being so prickly because her pride was hurting? If Bill had been working and she'd been free of all her financial worries, would she have handled Owen and Jill differently? Would she be so defensive? Was she just indulging in a fit of extremely large sour grapes?

'Definitely not. Most definitely not, Kate!' Anna, her other next-door

19

neighbour, said firmly when Kate, shame-faced, put this notion to her. She had told her friend of her encounter with Owen earlier that afternoon.

'The pushy shagger. The *nerve* of him going on about you saving electricity! If he comes near my garden with his lawnmower, I'll give him his answer. Who does he think he is, the Lord of the Estate? Those Kents are as thick as two short planks. It's obvious they're not used to money. Did you ever hear that Jill one trying to put on the posh accent? I'm telling you, they're the greatest pair of snobs going. If I didn't dislike them so much, I'd feel sorry for them. They haven't a clue! Just listen to Superdad, would you?' She nodded towards Owen, who was out in the middle of the street with a gang of kids. He was organising races.

'Now, Gemma, you stand there, just a little ahead of Jessica, Maria and Laura. And you, Jason, stay a bit behind. Matthew, Rachel and Patrick, stay where you are,' he instructed. 'On your marks . . .'

'Did you ever see the huge odds he gives to his own pair?' Anna murmured. 'Come on, kids. Beat those two little horrors,' she muttered as the race began.

'It's not really their fault.' Kate grinned as she watched Gemma and Jason trying to burst a gut to win the race. 'I mean, he keeps telling them how wonderful they are. Of course, naturally they believe it. And our lot just love to bring them down a peg or two.'

'I know. It brings out the nastiness in me, watching the carry-on of your man. Last weekend, young Jason came to the door, all togged out in his rugby gear. He asked John to come out and play a game of rugby with himself and Big Daddy. 'Thanks,' says John. 'I'm a soccer man myself.' He's not a bit impressed with any of their bull. Oh, to be an eight-year-old again.' Anna laughed as Owen roared at his son and daughter, urging them on to win the race.

'Brilliant race, Jase and Gems,' they heard him brag.

'Just pass me the sick bucket,' Anna said, before heading off to get the children's tea.

Kate didn't feel so bad about disliking the Kents after her chat with Anna. It wasn't just her difficult circumstances, or envy, that had put her off Owen and Jill and their offspring.

Time had not improved her feelings towards her neighbours. Right now, months later, she was fit to be tied as she stared down at her seven-year-old son. How *dare* Owen Kent talk about Bill's unemployment in front of Jason and Gemma?

'Mammy, *can* we go to EuroDisney some time?' Matthew's big blue eyes stared up into hers. They were wide and innocent and as blue as two cornflowers. 'Are you listening to me, Mammy?' Kate came to with a start.

'Of course I'm listening to you, pet. Some day, please God, we'll get to EuroDisney. We'll just have to say a prayer that Daddy gets a job soon. Never mind what Jason Kent says. We're not poor. We're very, very lucky to have a lovely house like this and a very special family.'

Matthew trotted off saying sweetly, 'Dear Holy God, please let my daddy get a job soon so he can bring us to EuroDisney before scummy Jason Kent goes.'

That had been a few days ago. Matthew hadn't mentioned it again. But as Kate gave her worktops one last wipe, she thought sadly that it wasn't a prayer they needed to get them to EuroDisney . . . it was a miracle.

Three

Kate sighed and gave a little shiver as she walked into the sitting-room. The house was cold. She felt so angry and frustrated that she could no longer just flick a switch and have instant heat. They had tried to save oil by turning on the heat later in the evenings. But winter had come early this year and they had run out of oil a week ago. Since then, Kate had been lighting the fire. Because they were economising on coal, the back boiler was never hot enough to give more than lukewarm heat to the radiators. With Christmas and all its expenses, they wouldn't be able to afford oil until well into the New Year. If even then.

I'm sick of this, Kate thought bitterly as she walked over to the floor-to-ceiling window. She stared out at the grey sky that promised snow.

Snow! That was all they needed to make life even more miserable. She was seriously thinking of looking for a job. She had been a legal secretary when she had married Bill. Maybe she should have stayed working. Then they wouldn't be so hard hit now. But if she got a job now, it would affect Bill's means-tested dole money. So the salary would have to be pretty good.

Who is going to employ an ex legal secretary with rusty secretarial skills, who isn't very computer literate? Kate thought unhappily as she straightened the folds in her net curtains. She had washed them yesterday and they were pristine white. Most of the other houses on their street had roller blinds. Net curtains were rather old fashioned. Kate had always liked 'proper curtains', as her grandmother called them. She hated the idea of people being able to see through her front window. Her home was her haven, not a showpiece for the neighbours to view every time they walked by.

Owen, whose latest quirk was practising his putting shots on the front lawn, was always trying to gawk in the window. It gave Kate no small satisfaction to know that he couldn't see in. Her curtains were her protection from his prying eyes. He was out now, strimming the edges of the lawn. She grinned as the catgut broke and flew across the grass. It was ridiculous—strimming edges at this time of the year. Kate frowned. She knew she was being petty, but she didn't care. He just got on her nerves. She had got so fed up of him strolling in front of her windows and playing rugby with Jason on the front lawn that she had asked her brother for advice. He was a gardener. He had planted a thorny orange-berried hedge, trained along a low white wooden fence, to separate the gardens and keep her unwanted neighbour out.

Jason was driving poor Matthew mad about the new computer he was getting for Christmas. It was going to be 'the best computer in the world', with better games than anyone else's, according to Jason. Every mother on the street could cheerfully have wrung Jason Kent's neck, as her own child demanded a 'best computer' as well.

That was what Bill and Kate had been arguing about this morning. What to buy the children for Christmas? Bill was as sick of penny pinching as she was. He wanted to borrow a couple of hundred quid from the credit union to splash out on Christmas and to hell with it. Kate had argued that they needed oil. The house insurance was coming up. The children all needed new shoes. If there was one thing Kate was particular about, it was getting good shoes for her children. A pair of decent shoes for a three-year-old could cost thirty or forty euro. Pay out forty euro each for the three of them and there wouldn't be much change out of a hundred and twenty smackers.

'We can't afford it and that's that,' Kate asserted. Bill's face darkened with frustration.

'Don't rub it in, for God's sake! I know we can't! I just want to give the kids a decent Christmas. Is that too much to want to do?' he snarled.

Kate sizzled. It wasn't *her* fault that they had no money. She was only trying to keep them out of debt.

'Listen, mister. You can do what you damn well like. I was only trying to help. Do you think *I* don't want to give them a good Christmas? I'm trying to do my best for all of us and it's not easy. So don't you take it out on me, Bill Ryan. It's not *my* fault that you're unemployed. It's not *me* who can't get a job.' Kate was so angry her voice was shaking. Months of suppressed rage, fear and frustration fuelled her outburst.

'You really know how to put the boot in, don't you?' Bill raged. 'You should have married someone like bloody Superdad over there, not a loser like me.' With that, he picked up his coat and strode out the front door. He slammed it hard behind him.

Sick at heart, Kate sat down at the kitchen table. She put her head in her hands and bawled her eyes out. She had never felt so sorry for herself. What had she done to deserve this? After twenty minutes of cursing and sobbing, she felt somewhat better. A good cry was just the thing sometimes. It helped to get it all out of your system. Luckily the children had spent the previous night with their cousins so they hadn't heard the row. She didn't want them upset as well.

It was almost three now, Kate noted, and still no sign of Bill. She wondered what he was doing. It had got even darker outside. The clouds were so low they seemed to touch the rooftops. The frost, which hadn't thawed all day, cast a silvery sheen on the lawns. The flaming orange of the hedge's berries were a startling contrast. The stark shapes of leafless trees in the gardens gave a wintry air. Smoke curled from several chimneys. A robin nestled in the shelter of an evergreen shrub. A clump of colourful bachelors' buttons under the hedge added cheer to the cold, dull day. They were her favourite flower. Normally Kate would have enjoyed the pretty wintry scene outside her big window. But today it just seemed bleak and cold. She shivered again.

'To hell with it,' she muttered crossly. With a determined set to her jaw, she walked over to the fire and struck a match. She watched with pleasure as the flames licked the firelighters and roared up the chimney. The sticks caught fire and, spitting and sparking, scented the room with the freshness of pine. The glow of the orange and yellow flames casting their shadows on the walls soothed Kate.

With a deep sigh, she sat cross-legged on the rug in front of the fire. She pulled two large carrier bags overflowing with presents in front of her. This was the ideal time to sort out the Christmas-present situation. It was something she had been putting off all day. She might as well sort it while Bill and the kids were out of the house. If she was quick and organised, she'd be finished before he came home. Then her husband wouldn't have the added embarrassment of seeing her sort presents they'd received last year, to give to their relatives this year. If only she could remember who had given her what. It would be a disaster to return a gift to someone who had given it to them in the first place.

Kate gave a wry smile as she unloaded the bags onto the floor. The only other time in her life she had had to recycle presents was that first year she had moved into a flat with her two best friends. They had all been broke. It had been fun then, though, not like this.

She eyed the collection surrounding her. Table mats. They could go to Aunt Ella. A basket of Body Shop soaps and shampoos. Now, who had given her those? She cast her mind back. Was it Sally? No. It was Rita, her sister-in-law. Well, Sally could have the Body Shop basket. Rita could have the lovely white angora scarf that Karen, a good friend, had given her. Kate fingered the scarf, enjoying the feel of the soft wool between her fingers. It would have been nice to be able to wear it herself, she thought regretfully. But needs must, and Rita would like it. She wanted to give her sister-in-law a nice present. Rita was very good to them, as were all of their families.

That was why Kate wanted to give them presents at Christmas. And she wanted to show that she and Bill were not completely on their uppers. This year, she decided, she would keep a list of who gave what. That way, if Bill was still unemployed next Christmas, it would be easier for her to match up presents. If people saw her this minute, no doubt they would think she was dreadfully mean. But it was the best she could do under the circumstances. She spent a peaceful hour sitting in the fire's glow sorting out the presents.

She had just stood up, trying to get rid of the pins and needles in her feet, when she saw Bill marching down the street. He was lugging the biggest, bushiest Christmas tree she had ever seen. A broad grin creased her face. Bill was a sucker for Christmas trees. The bigger and bushier, the better.

She flung open the front door as her husband struggled up the path with his load. Panting, he stood looking at her.

'I'm sorry, love. I didn't mean it.' Their eyes met. 'You're the best wife a man could have and I know I'm dead lucky.'

'Oh, Bill, it's all right. I didn't mean what I said either,' Kate assured him, happy that their little tiff was over. She flung her arms around him and the tree and was rewarded with a one-armed bear hug. 'It's brilliant! Where did you get it?' She looked at the tree admiringly.

'Down the town from a bloke on a lorry. Look at the width of it. And look at the fullness up top. The symmetry is almost perfect.' Bill, who was a good judge of Christmas trees, enthused about his find. 'It's the best ever.'

'You say that every year,' Kate laughed. 'Come on in. I have the fire lighting. It was cold, so I lit it early so the place will be warm when the kids get home,' she added a little defensively.

'You did right, Kate. It's bloody freezing out today,' Bill agreed. They smiled at each other. His eyes lit up. 'What if I rang Rita and asked her to keep the kids for another hour or two? Then we could decorate the tree for them as a surprise.'

'Great idea! Just imagine their faces.' Kate felt her previous sadness lift. A rare light-hearted mood enveloped her. 'Do you think Rita would mind?'

'No.' Bill shook his head. 'We'll take her gang if she wants to go shopping tomorrow.'

'Right,' Kate said briskly. 'You ring her and I'll put the kettle on. We'll have a cup of coffee and get going.' Unemployment be damned. They were going to have the best Christmas tree ever.

Rita willingly agreed to keep the

children for another couple of hours. She gratefully agreed to let Kate take her own children the following afternoon so she could do some Sunday shopping in peace.

For the next two hours Kate and Bill totally enjoyed themselves. They transformed the six-foot tree into a magical delight, adorned with twinkling lights, glittering ornaments and frothy tinsel. They laced the ceiling with garlands and Kate prepared the crib. She twined ivy across the top and down the sides of the little wooden structure. She fixed up a small light to shine on the figures. She laid the straw that she kept, year after year, on the floor of the crib. Bill hung up a sheriff's star from an old cowboy set that he had had as a child. It glittered in the firelight, as bright as any star of Bethlehem. Finally, Kate gently placed the figures of Mary and Joseph inside the crib. At their feet, she put the ox and the ass. She arranged the three wise men and the shepherd at the entrance. All that remained was for the infant Jesus, lying in his manger, to be placed in the crib. They would have a little ceremony when the children were home. Jessica, being the youngest, would put Baby Jesus in the crib.

They stood back to admire their work. 'It's lovely,' Bill said, as Kate fussed at a piece of ivy, wanting to have it just so.

'So is the tree.' Kate smiled. 'Definitely the best ever.'

'It's a biggie all right.' Bill grinned.

'Bigger than Superdad's,' Kate murmured wickedly. Bill laughed.

'And real as well. Poor Jason has to make do with an artificial one, even if it *is* the biggest and most expensive one there is. It's just not the same, sure it isn't?' His eyes twinkled. Owen and Jill had put their tree up over a week ago. They had been the first in the street to put one up.

Great wreaths of holly hung on their door and windows. Jason and Gemma were bursting with pride.

Each day, Matthew asked anxiously if they were going to put their tree up this year. And Kate reassured her young son that, yes, they would be putting one up. She was dying to see his face when he saw the six-foot giant that now stood twinkling in their front window.

They were starving after their effort. They decided they deserved a treat so they ordered a Chinese. They ate it sitting in front of the fire, enjoying spare ribs in barbecue sauce, crispy duck and prawn crackers. The sparkling lights of the Christmas tree, and the amber glow of the fire, enveloped them in a cocoon of golden warmth. Rain and sleet lashed against the windows. The wind howled down the chimney. Kate and Bill cuddled and chatted and enjoyed their fireside picnic. They put their troubles behind them for the precious few hours they had to themselves. It was one of the nicest evenings they'd had in a long, long time.

Four

An hour later, with the lights of the tree switched off and the sitting-room in darkness, they heard Rita's car in the drive. The children tumbled out of the car and ran in out of the rain. 'I won't come in,' Rita yelled, sticking her head out the window. 'I'll see you tomorrow around two, with my gang.'

'Fine, Rita, thanks a million,' Kate called back as Bill helped the kids take off their coats and hats. She was glad to close the door and shut out the bitterly cold night.

'We have a surprise for you. You've got to close your eyes, and no peeping,' Bill warned as he led Rachel, Matthew and Jessica to the sitting-room door.

'What is it? What is it?' Matthew hopped from one leg to the other with impatience.

'Matthew, they're not going to tell you because it won't be a surprise then,' Rachel said, doing her big sister act. But Kate could see her eyes sparkling with anticipation.

'Hurry on.' Jessica had her fingers up to her eyes. She peered through them. Watching the antics of the three of them, Kate experienced a moment of happiness. She knew that, whatever happened in the future, no one could take these precious moments away from her.

'Keep those eyes shut,' Bill said as Kate took Jessica by the hand. She led the way into the darkened sitting-room, lit only by the firelight and the little red lamp in the crib.

'Open up!' Bill ordered as he plugged in the lights. He smiled happily at Kate as the children squealed with delight and excitement.

'Oh Daddy, it's MEGA!' Matthew was bursting with pride.

'Oh Mammy, isn't it *beautiful*?' Rachel sighed. Jessica stood speechless, her big blue eyes getting rounder by the minute. Gently, she stretched out a chubby little hand and touched one of the ornaments.

'Santa Claus!' she exclaimed, stroking the little fat Santa, her eyes as bright as the Christmas-tree lights.

'Oh, look at the crib, Mammy. Can we put the baby Jesus in?' Rachel begged.

'Daddy and I were waiting until you came home so we could welcome Baby Jesus into our family.' Kate hugged her eldest daughter. She wanted her children to understand and appreciate the spirituality of Christmas. The crib ceremony was one of their most important family events.

With great earnestness, Rachel placed the little figure of Jesus in his manger in her younger sister's hands. She helped the toddler to place it in the centre of the straw, between Mary and Joseph.

'Welcome, Baby Jesus,' they all chorused reverently.

'And we hope you'll be very comfortable in your manger,' Rachel added as she patted the straw down. Jessica planted a big wet kiss on the newly installed infant.

'I bet he *will* be comfortable. Our crib is *much* nicer than Jason Kent's and they don't have a light, or straw, either,' Matthew declared. He took a wisp of straw and placed it in front of the two little sheep. 'In case they're hungry,' he explained to his parents, who were having a very hard time keeping their faces straight.

The following Monday morning, Bill arrived upstairs with a cup of early morning tea for his wife. 'What kind of a day is it?' Kate murmured sleepily. She and Bill were going shopping for the Santa toys. They had decided on a compromise. They were going to borrow €150 from the credit union. They also had a little nest egg that Kate had managed to put by especially for Christmas. She'd saved it out of her children's allowance.

Through a chink in the curtains she could see a sliver of brightness. The wind of the previous two days had died down. She sat up in bed and sipped the hot, sweet tea. Bill drew back the curtains and peered out.

'I don't believe it,' she heard him say. 'Kate, come here. You've just got to see this!'

'What?' she asked. She set her cup on the bedside locker and hopped out of bed, shivering in the frosty air. She snuggled into her fleecy dressing gown and looked where her husband was pointing.

Kate burst out laughing. 'What a prat! What a prize prat. He must have been up at six putting that up. It wasn't there last night. He had to try

and outdo us. What a sad little man.'
She giggled as she viewed an
outsized fir tree, decorated with
multi-coloured lights, standing in a
tub in the centre of the Kents' front
lawn.

Five

All in all, it hadn't been a bad Christmas, Kate decided. She was putting the finishing touches to the home-made soup she was serving as a starter for lunch with Carmel. It was made with the remains of the turkey and there was eating and drinking in it. There'd be plenty for tomorrow, she thought with satisfaction.

It was the day after Stephen's Day. Bill had taken the children into Dublin on the DART, to go to the pictures. Kate and her friend would have time to themselves. Kate had lit the fire early. They were going through coal at an awful rate. Once the children were back at school, it would be back to lighting a fire in the evening. Still, at least the house was warm for her guest today. The icing on the cake was the tank full of oil, which was a Christmas gift from her parents. She'd had the heating on earlier and she'd timed it to come on later in the evening. The house was as warm as toast. Carmel wouldn't know they were experiencing hard times.

They had gone to secondary school together. They'd both got jobs and got their first flat together. Then Carmel had fallen in love with a doctor. They had married and gone to live in Dubai.

Kate kept in touch by letter and the occasional phone call and then, in the last couple of years, by e-mail. Carmel had come back home several times over the years. Kate had marvelled at how glamorous and sophisticated her friend had become. Carmel had a glittering lifestyle out in the Emirates. A life full of parties and shopping and exotic travel. Carmel's husband, Peter, was a successful consultant. Kate had got to know Peter when he was dating

Carmel. She had found him to be a very charming and cultured man.

She lifted the lid of the saucepan simmering alongside the soup. The pungent aroma of korma filled the air. She'd put the remains of the turkey meat into it and had added plenty of onion, sultanas and cream. Thank God for Uncle Ben's chicken korma sauce, she thought as she gave the mixture a stir. Her mother had made a Christmas pudding for her. Her mother-in-law had made a cake. So at least she had dessert and afternoon tea taken care of. She also had a good bottle of wine chilling. Someone had given it to her ages ago and she had put it aside for a special occasion. This was just such an occasion.

It was just as well Carmel had picked the day after Stephen's Day to visit because there was very little left in the kitty. What was in the fridge was going to have to do them for the rest of the week. Still, Rachel and Matthew had been thrilled with their new bikes. Jessica was playing her ABC computer morning, noon and night. It had been a good idea to put those few euros from the children's allowance aside over the year. It had gone a long way towards paying for their Santa gifts.

Kate turned down the bubbling sauce and went to give a last look over the house. She had hoovered and dusted that morning. The house was fragrant with polish. A thought struck her. She ran upstairs to her bedroom and opened her wardrobe. On the shelf beside her make-up, there was a three-quarter-full roll of soft, green toilet paper. Kate took it into the bathroom and replaced the rough, off-white thrift roll that was in the toilet-roll holder. Maybe she was being daft, but she badly wanted to keep up appearances. She always kept an expensive roll for visitors. There was no need for Carmel to know anything about Bill being unemployed.

She couldn't explain why she didn't want her friend to know of their bad luck. Carmel wouldn't look down her nose at them in the least. She wasn't a bit like that, for all her wealth. She'd be very sympathetic, if anything. It was just her silly pride, Kate decided. But Bill's unemployment seemed almost equal to failure in comparison to Peter's success and wealth. It was a horrible thing to think. She scolded herself, shame-faced, but even so . . .

Just for good measure, she produced a box of matching tissues that she was also keeping for 'good wear'. She placed them on the shelf under the mirror. Satisfied, Kate went back downstairs to await her guest. She paused in front of the mirror to check how she looked. She'd got her hair cut and blow-dried on Christmas Eve and it still looked good. A touch of make-up did wonders. The new Egyptian

Shimmer that her sister had given her was very flattering.

The last year had added a few grey hairs to her chestnut curls, she thought. The fine lines around her wide hazel eyes had deepened. Still, she didn't look too bad, considering. The cream pants and amber blouse looked very well on her. A ring on the doorbell made her jump. She glanced at her watch. Carmel was early.

Six

'Happy Christmas,' Carmel smiled as Kate flung open the door. They hugged warmly. Carmel was certainly dressed for the weather in a beautiful leather coat and furry hat and scarf.

'Come in, come in.' Now that she was here, Kate was delighted to see her.

'God above, I'm freezing!' Carmel shivered as she shut the door behind her.

'I've a blazing fire lighting. Come and sit down beside it,' Kate urged, leading the way into the sitting-room.

'I've been cold since I came home,' Carmel explained. 'The heat thins your blood. I've two thermal vests on.' She hung her coat on the hall stand. She looked tired, Kate thought. Her make-up was perfectly applied and her blonde, streaked hair, worn up, was very elegant.

'Well, how are you, Kate, and how have things been? Tell me all the news,' Carmel said as she sank into the big armchair in front of the fire. She held out her hands to the blaze.

'I'm fine, we're all fine,' Kate said cheerfully. 'Now sit down there and relax. What will you have to drink?'

'I have the car, Kate, so I'll just have one glass of wine,' Carmel replied. Kate gave a mental sigh of relief. The good wine would last through lunch. She wouldn't have to open that awful bottle of plonk she'd bought on special offer. She should have remembered that Carmel always hired a car when she was home. She went to the kitchen to pour the wine.

'There's a lovely smell.' Carmel had followed her in. 'What's for lunch?'

'Homemade soup. Korma with Caesar salad and garlic bread. And plum pudding with custard and brandy butter,' Kate answered as she did the business with the corkscrew.

'Very nice, Kate.' Carmel lifted the lid of the saucepan and sniffed. 'I've really been looking forward to seeing you and catching up on all the news and gossip. Where are Bill and the children?'

Kate handed her a glass of wine. 'He took them into Dublin on the DART, for a treat. They've gone to the pictures.' Carmel's face fell.

'I will get to see them, won't I?'

'Oh, indeed you will,' laughed Kate.

'Oh good. I've brought them a few presents. I've a bottle of brandy for yourself and Bill too.'

'Carmel, you shouldn't have,' Kate exclaimed. Her friend was very good like that. Knowing that Carmel wouldn't come empty handed, Kate had wrapped up a copy of best-selling author Cathy Kelly's new novel. Her Aunt Ella had given it to her. She'd been dying to read it herself but she knew that Carmel, who was an avid reader, would enjoy it. And it was a decent present to give to her old friend. She'd also given her a boxed set of ivory candles that she'd kept from last year.

'I suppose I won't recognise the children.' Carmel sipped her wine and began to relax. 'Jessica wasn't walking the last time I was home.'

'She's well and truly walking now and up to all kinds of mischief.' Kate took a sip of her wine. Carmel had no children, but she took a great interest in Rachel, Matthew and Jessica. She always brought them gifts on her trips home from Dubai.

'Will I serve up our lunch now?' Kate asked her friend after they had chatted for a while.

'Why not?' Carmel agreed.

'Go on into the dining-room and sit down and I'll bring in the soup,' Kate instructed. She had the dining table set with the good silverware and crystal and her best linen tablecloth and napkins. And she had a lovely centrepiece on the table. A creation of holly and ivy entwined around gold and silver balls and a pair of red candles. She lit the candles and served the soup and the two of them sat down to continue their chat.

Although Carmel had said she was peckish, she didn't eat much. Kate was worried that perhaps she hadn't liked the korma. Her friend always ate like a horse and never put on an ounce. Kate only had to look at a cream cake to put on weight.

'Was it OK? Maybe it was a bit spicy?' she asked.

'No, no! It was fine. Really!' Carmel assured her. 'I just wasn't as hungry as I thought.'

They drank their coffee at the fire. Kate, listening to tales of the glamorous life in the Emirates, couldn't bring herself to tell Carmel that Bill was unemployed. He and the children arrived home a little later. They were full of talk about their jaunt on the DART and their trip to the cinema.

'It's lovely and warm in here,' Matthew said happily. Kate prayed that her son would say nothing else. She didn't want her wealthy friend to know that the house wasn't always this warm.

When Carmel produced their presents, there was great excitement. It was like Christmas morning all over again. Carmel was in her element as they all vied for hugs and kisses. After a while, Bill took the three of them out to the kitchen to give them some hot turkey soup. Rachel, on her way out the door, said wistfully, 'I wish it was Christmas every day of the year so we could always have this yummy food.'

Kate nearly died. Her face actually burned as she waited for her child to say that she was sick of mince and fish fingers and rice. But Rachel said nothing else and skipped after her sister and brother.

'Turkey and ham and Christmas pud always seem so exotic when you're a child, don't they?' Carmel remarked innocently, unaware of Kate's dismay.

'Hmm,' agreed Kate distractedly. God only knew what the children were going to come out with next. She should have been honest with Carmel at the beginning and told her about Bill being unemployed. There was no shame in it. It could happen to anyone. But it would look a bit odd if she suddenly blurted it out now. Especially when she'd led Carmel to believe that everything was normal in the Ryan household. She was going to be on edge for the rest of the evening. She must try and get Bill on his own for a minute and tell him to say nothing about being unemployed. She'd tell him she'd explain later. He'd probably be annoyed with her. Perhaps he'd feel that she was ashamed of him. She'd made a right mess of things by trying to keep up appearances, she thought miserably.

'They're just gorgeous, Kate. You're so lucky,' Carmel said wistfully, unaware of her friend's distress.

'I know,' Kate agreed. She carefully folded up the expensive wrapping paper. It would come in handy next year.

'Mammy, I did a wee-wee all by myself.' Jessica appeared at the door with her dress caught up in her little panties.

'You're a great girl!' her mother exclaimed. 'Come here until I tuck in your vest.' Jessica cuddled in against her as Kate adjusted her clothing.

'There's lovely soft toilet roll in the bathroom. It's nice and soft on my bum-bum,' Jessica announced, staring at Carmel.

God above! Kate thought in embarrassment. Next she'll be saying we're poor people or something.

Flustered, she told her daughter to go back out to the kitchen to finish her soup. Jessica wrapped her little arms around her neck.

'I love you, Mammy. The next time will you come to the pictures?'

'Of course I will, love.' Kate hugged the little girl to her before she went trotting out to the kitchen.

'She's so beautiful,' Carmel said. She sounded terribly sad. Kate caught her friend's gaze. To her dismay, she saw that Carmel's eyes were bright with tears.

Seven

'What's wrong, Carmel?' Kate hurried to close the door before rushing to her side. 'What is it? Tell me what's wrong.' She put her arms around her upset friend.

'Me and Peter, we're finished. He's been having an affair with my best friend, Elaine, out in Dubai. And now he wants a divorce. Can you believe it?' Carmel sobbed. 'They've been deceiving me for years. It's been going on all through our marriage. She was always so sweet to me, the lying little bitch.'

'That's terrible!' Kate couldn't believe it. Peter had always seemed like the perfect husband. Imagine sleeping with your best friend's husband! That was the pits. Elaine wasn't much of a friend, Kate reflected. No real friend would do that, no matter how strong the

61

attraction.

'I didn't want to tell you. I was just too ashamed,' Carmel gulped. 'I don't know why *I* should be ashamed. I did nothing to be ashamed about. It's just . . . Oh, you know what I mean, Kate? Then when I saw how happy you are with Bill and those beautiful children, I felt I just couldn't tell you. Can you understand?' she hiccupped.

'I understand exactly,' Kate said slowly. 'Actually, Carmel, I've been keeping something from you as well.' She met her friend's tear-stained gaze. 'Bill's been out of work for over eighteen months and it's a real struggle. Like you, I couldn't bring myself to say it out straight. I'm sorry. It was just silly pride.'

'What idiots we are!' Carmel gave a shaky grin. 'But that's awful for you and Bill. At least the pair of you are as crazy about each other as ever. You can spot that a mile off. I was so gutted when I found out about Peter and that . . . that pea-brained cow. No wonder he wouldn't agree to have children. Every time I suggested trying for a baby he said to wait another year. He didn't want his cushy lifestyle disrupted by crying babies. Wives and mistresses are enough to cope with. There's been more than Elaine, you know. He's been screwing around left, right and centre it seems. I even went for an Aids test after his sordid little confession, when I found out what he was up to. Imagine! I'll probably never have a child of my own now.' Her voice wobbled and she burst into tears again.

'Of course you will. You'll meet someone. You're still a young woman,' Kate soothed, shocked by what she had just heard. Her own circumstances might not be the best. But they were a hell of a lot better than Carmel's. No wonder the poor girl couldn't eat her lunch. No wonder she seemed so on edge this afternoon.

'I haven't told the family yet. Ma will have a fit to think I'm getting a divorce. Imagine what the neighbours will say.'

'Don't mind the blooming neighbours,' Kate retorted.

'It's such a relief to tell someone, Kate,' Carmel confessed, wiping her eyes with the back of her hand. 'It's been so hard being at home and everyone thinking everything's normal.'

'Of course it's been hard, Carmel. But you've got to tell them. You can't go around keeping that to yourself. You'd crack up. And I know your family. They'll be very supportive. It's amazing how kind people are when the chips are down. I know.'

'Oh Kate, what idiots we've been trying to put on brave faces. If we can't tell each other our problems, then who can we tell?' Carmel said.

'Exactly!' Kate agreed. 'Now look, why don't you phone home and tell them you're staying the night? We'll open the brandy you brought and have a really good natter about things.'

'Kate, that would be lovely,' Carmel sighed, beginning to feel better already.

'I'll just put the heat on in the spare bedroom, and fish out some towels and a clean night-dress for you.'

'Now, don't go to any trouble,' Carmel warned.

'It's no trouble for an old pal,' Kate said firmly.

She switched on the radiator and laid a clean, long-sleeved nightdress on Carmel's bed. That would keep her snug, she thought. She'd put the electric blanket on later. To hell with the electricity bill for once. Carmel was going through a bad enough time without spending the night shivering in bed.

Kate stood at the bedroom window staring out into the night. A sliver of new moon hid behind a wisp of cloud. The lights of the Christmas trees in the windows glittered magically. Owen's outdoor fir tree stood proudly on his front lawn. Lit up for all to see. Owen had bought a second-hand SUV for Christmas. He'd spent a lot of time sitting in it making calls on his mobile phone. Kate smiled. He was pathetically childish really. Maybe there was some reason for his immature behaviour. Maybe he'd had a terribly deprived childhood. Who knew? Who knew what went on in people's lives? Look at poor Carmel. Who would have believed it? No matter what, she and Bill were lucky. They had each other and they had the children. She pulled the curtains, straightened their folds, switched off the light and went downstairs.

Jessica was sitting on Carmel's knee. Carmel was reading *The Little Match Girl* to her. Jessica was engrossed.

'You know, Kate, I've just had a brainwave. You and I and Bill are going to have a good chat once the darlings are in bed.' Carmel's eyes sparkled.

'What are you up to?' Kate knew her friend well.

'Patience, my dear,' Carmel said calmly and resumed her storytelling.

Eight

'Bill, how would you like to go into business with me?' Carmel asked later that evening, as they sipped the brandy she'd brought. 'I'm going to start importing antique furniture from the Orient. You can get the most magnificent pieces out there. As well as rugs and throws. I've hundreds of contacts from all the years I've been out there. It's something I've been thinking about since I found out about Peter and Elaine. People always admire the pieces I have here in Dublin. I think I could, with good marketing, make a go of it. Would you be interested in coming on board?'

'It sounds good,' Bill said cautiously. 'But you're going to need a base here, at the very least. Property prices are sky high.'

Carmel smiled broadly. 'Bill, my

darling rat of a husband was full of clever ideas about evading tax here. He bought one of those big houses off Stephen's Green years ago when the market was bad. He put it in my name. He's not getting it back! Legally it's mine. All the paperwork is in my name. All the money from the rent goes into an account in my name. It's invested in Post Office Bonds. Tax free!' Carmel's mouth tightened. 'He's not getting it back. He's picked the wrong woman to cheat on. What goes around comes around. If he makes a fuss I'm going to rat on him to the tax inspectors. He has accounts all over the place. That will frighten the living daylights out of him. So I don't think he'll argue. He has too much to lose.

'I'm going to use the top floor for offices. I'll make show rooms out of the rest of the house. I'm going to make a fortune and he can go take a hike. Success is the best revenge. Are you in?'

'Why not?' Bill felt a tingle of excitement. This could work.

Carmel looked over at Kate. 'We'll need a secretary. It will be like old times.'

Kate laughed. 'Sounds good to me. I can still type . . . just about.'

'It's going to be exciting.' Carmel's eyes gleamed. 'I can't wait to get going.'

'Me too.' Bill sat up straight. 'Let's start working on a rough business plan.'

'Hold on, I'll make us a pot of coffee to sober us up,' giggled Kate. 'I think I'm imagining all this.'

'No you're not, Kate. Tonight is the night when everything starts to go right for all of us again,' Carmel said firmly. 'I'll show that rat what I can do.'

Maybe her friend was right, Kate decided later as she lay in bed. Her head was buzzing with ideas. Beside her, Bill snored contentedly. To think she'd been dreading her friend's visit. And Carmel had been dreading telling her about her marriage break-up. If they hadn't confided in each other, the chance to start over might never have presented itself. Maybe it was going to be the best year ever. Bill and she would be working again. Carmel was a very dynamic woman. And she was driven. She would make a go of this business, do or die. Her husband would only be able to stand by and watch. Kate knew her friend well. Peter would rue the day he cheated on her.

Kate turned over and put her arm around Bill. They had a sound and happy marriage. She loved him very much and he loved her. They had that comfort. Carmel might have clothes and jewels and great wealth, but she was deeply unhappy.

Kate knew she was the lucky one. At least if the business took off, Carmel would have something to occupy her while she came to terms with her husband's betrayal. And it *was* going to take off. Kate felt a surge of optimism. There was light at the end of the tunnel and she was full of hope.